# The Ghost of Zak Brady

by Ciaran McLaughlin

# THE GHOST
# OF ZAK BRADY

**Ciaran McLaughlin**

| Printed in the United States of America | |
| --- | --- |
| Library of Congress Control Number: | 0-9000000-0-0 |
| ISBN: Softcover | 978-1-964331-07-2 |
| e-Book | 0-9000000-0-0 |

Republished by: Ciaran McLaughlin

Publication Date: 2025

To order copies of this book, contact:

Ciaran McLaughlin

Phone: 0868830296
Email: ciaranmcl1972@gmail.com

# CONTENTS

# DEDICATION

To my wife, sons, daughter, mum, brothers and in-laws. In memory of my sister Marianne. I am eternally grateful to have shared your thoughts, wisdom, wit and stories. I would like to dedicate my first book to you all. Oh, and thanks to myself for finally finishing this book after so many years of writing it.

I would like to dedicate this book to my former English teacher, Mr. Conboy, who gave me the freedom to express myself, the belief and imagination to bring characters to life. Thanks, sir, for your creative genius.

I would like to dedicate this book to Emily Daly. Thanks for your wisdom, honesty and your incredible knowledge.

# ACKNOWLEDGEMENT

I am extremely grateful to Enda McCallion for believing in my story and dreams. A sincere thanks for all your support and encouragement. This book would not be completed without your coaxing. A massive thanks also to my brother Gary for his sketches and help throughout this book, your help has already proved invaluable. The completion of my first book would not have been possible without the support and nurturing of Patricia and Jhecris at Doxa Literary House LLC.

*Ciaran McLaughlin*

# *"Voices from the Grave "*

Zak Brady is a 15-year-old teenage boy who lives and breathes football, he is an only child to parents Roy and Molly. He yearns for a brother but the closest he gets is his childhood friend Lee O'Brien. Both teenagers attend Mountmear College just 4 miles from Oakheart, they both play for the school team and they are going well in the league and cup but face their bitter rivals Oakheart Rovers in the semi-finals. Zak is also mad about Sarah Jessica the coach's daughter, he is besotted with her especially her long blonde hair and deep blue eyes, he has never felt this way about anyone in his life before.

Zak is standing in the centre circle, daydreaming of Sarah Jessica when he hears a wispy, eerie-sounding voice saying' Get to the penalty spot "Get to the penalty spot" Zak duly obliges and scores his team a crucial goal against their deadly rivals Oakheart Rovers. Zak looks around and sees this young boy with auburn hair and freckles cheering him from the sidelines, zak looks again and the boy is gone, just disappeared leaving Zak puzzled and confused.

Who is this young boy who is helping him from the sidelines and why is he here?

Zak's life is going great, he's enjoying school (for a change) his school team are in the final of the Enda Tolley Cup and is second in the league. Sarah Jessica and Zak are getting closer and closer when inside 60 seconds, Zak's world comes crashing down when he learns that Sarah Jessica has been rushed to hospital with a serious illness. Zak loses all interest in school, football and life. His heart is breaking and he can't understand why this is happening. Months and months pass when finally Zak gets the news that Sarah Jessica has made a miraculous recovery. Zak's eyes light up, his smile is back and he rushes to the hospital to be with the love of his life. He embraces Sarah Jessica for ages and they both share happy tears.

The final of the cup is played and it is a very tight affair when Zak pops up at the death to score the winner, he is always in the right place at the right time, unknown to others Jack O'Leary ( Zak's ghost) is speaking to Zak and telling him what to do and where to go. The league is coming to an end and it's the final game with 2 teams still with a chance of winning the league, Oakheart celtic and Mountmear the 2 best teams in the league.

Zak pops up again with the winner for his team and they clinch the league title on goal difference by just 1 goal. The Ghost of Zak Brady again gives great advice to his friend.

Oakheart Celtic win the double, league and cup in the same year, what an achievement.

Jack tells Zak that he has to leave as his time is up and Zak is devastated, where are you going? Are you coming back? Jack winks and says I hope to and then he disappears into the fog that covers the pitch.

# *Foreword*

Zak Brady is a football-mad teenager who is an only child. He sometimes feels alone in the house, even with his mum and dad at home. Thankfully, his best friend since childhood, Lee O'Brien, is always on hand to play football outside and inside on Zak's computer. Zak longs to have another sibling, preferably a brother. Both boys attend Mountmear College and play on the school team. Zak is a gifted player, but in recent games, he has struggled to find his best form.

Zak starts to hear voices when he's on the pitch and is amazed when the voice tells him exactly where to be, he seems to be always in the right place at the right time. Zak soon learns that a boy with auburn hair is cheering him on from the sidelines and is also helping him to succeed. The coach's daughter Sarah Jessica is on Zak's mind night and day; he is smitten with her and has fallen for her in a big way, Zak finally plucks up the courage to ask her out on a date after weeks and months of trying.

The cup final is also on Zak's mind, and he is trying to juggle this along with school and now a romance.

Zak visits the library and investigates this mystery boy. he discovers that the boy's name is Jack O'Leary and he has been dead for the past 60 years. A ghost and he is talking to Zak.

Zack's life is turned upside down when he learns that Sarah Jessica is rushed to hospital and worse was to follow when he hears that the love of his young life has leukaemia. He loses interest in football, school and life in general. He was getting very, very close to Sarah Jessica, but his life is unravelling before his eyes, and he feels so helpless.

A few months pass, and Zak hears the news that he had been hoping and praying for. Sarah Jessica has made a miraculous recovery, and hearing this great news, Zak rushes to her to be at her bedside.

Oakheart Celtic plays Mountmear in the cup final, and it's a humdinger of a game. The match goes to the final minutes when Zak pops up with a crucial goal to defeat the favourites. Oakheart Celtic also went to the last league game holding a 1 goal advantage on goal difference. They won the game and the league, thanks again to Zak and his friend Jack O'Leary.

Zak's ghost friend, Jack, tells him that he has to leave and that his time is up. Zak has so many questions, but Jack hints that he may see him again.

# CHAPTER 1
## *Semi-Final*

90 minutes on the clock, in the far corner of the stadium, this semi-final cup match between bitter local rivals Oakheart Celtic and Oakheart rovers is moving closer to extra time. Zak gets to his feet after a strong tackle from the big centre half, who has marked him so closely all game.

"I heard you were good" the big number 5 quipped with a satisfying smirk on his face. "You'll see", replied Zak as he brushed into the defender with his shoulder.

The captain of Oakheart Celtic steps up to take the free-kick, It's just 25 yards out on the left-hand side of the box, Finn rook is the talisman of the team, He takes all the penalties, free-kicks and corner kicks, everything goes through him.

Zak makes his way into the box, he slowly walks backwards to the back post and is tightly marked by the number 5 from Oakheart Rovers, whose nickname is donkey! due to his strength and hard kicks.

He grabs hold of Zak's shirt and tries to wrestle him to the ground, Zak wriggles free and hears a voice saying," get to the penalty spot! Get to the penalty spot! Finn fires in a fierce free kick into the box.

Oakheart rovers number 2 jumps highest and heads the ball firmly out of the area, John Keaney, the right back, drives the ball back in, It deflects off the keeper's  shin, and the ball loops into the path of Zak, Who is moving towards the penalty spot?

He takes the ball down on his left knee and takes a quick look at the keeper, who is charging out from his line, Zak lifts the ball over the oncoming goalkeeper and side- foots the ball into the open net, The crowd erupt, and celebrations break out all over the stadium, Zak and his teammates sprint back to their half.

Zak and Lee are running together.

Zak: did you hear that?

Lee: hear what?

Zak: a voice. told me to get to the penalty spot. Lee: (laughs) you're as mad as a box of frogs, brady.

But if it speaks to you again, do exactly what it says.

Zak glances to the sideline and notices a boy with auburn hair, this boy has freckles on his face and long hair.

Zak gets back inside his half and looks over again, but the boy is gone, just disappeared into the trees".

He is utterly confused. The game restarts, and Zak is still looking for the boy with auburn hair.

Suddenly a loud roar is heard, "wake up, lad! wake up!" get back and help your team.

There is only one minute left! Coach Dempsey is barking orders to the boys.

Oakheart rovers are in a hurry, and they take a quick throw in, Aidan Wilson, the left back, rises highest and sends the ball back into rovers half, Where Finn Rook takes the ball down on his chest, swivels and switches the play to his twin brother Noah, The speedy number eleven has only one thing on his mind when he's running at the rovers' defence, he beats one challenge, nutmegs another and is ready to shoot when he gets clobbered by the number 4, that will slow you down, might even stop your wee tricks", the number 4 stands over Noah smirking, as he is lying flat out on his back.

Noah gets to his feet gingerly, Finn takes the free kick quickly and flicks the ball to Zak, Who is moving into the box, Zak hears the voice again, "Get to the edge of the box" "The edge of the box" Lee O'Brien, The number 6 who plays mostly on the opposite wing to Noah Rook.

Takes a touch and crosses the ball first time into the box, Tyrone Reilly, the big number 9, Jumps and heads the ball back to Zak brady, who is on the edge of the box, he meets the ball first time on the volley, Zak drives his laces through the ball, It blasts like a cannonball into the roof of the net.

The net bulges, the metal pins anchoring the net into the ground go flying.

The rovers' keeper dives full stretch but is unable to keep the ball out.

2-0 to celtic over their local arch-rivals. There's no way back now for Rovers.

Zak looks over to the sideline and is looking for the boy again. he spy's him at the side of the dugout, he's clapping and cheering as Zak thinks to himself, Who are you? Why are you helping me? the referee puts his whistle to his lips and gives 3 sharp blows, that's it, the match is over!

Oakheart Celtic are through to the final.

The away side slump to their knees, they have lost another semi-final and this one to their bitter rivals Oakheart Celtic.

The distraught is clear to see on their faces, on the other side of the pitch, the Celtic players are buzzing, they are jumping around, hugging each other and the smiles on their faces says it all.

Zak's teammates dive on top of him, the scene is euphoric. They are in the final!

The manager, Justin Dempsey, comes onto the pitch to congratulate the players.

He has a broad smile on his face, and he tells the players that he is very proud of them all today.

The coach calls over captain Finn Rook and whispers in his ear, Finn gathers the team in the semi-circle and gives a rousing speech that makes their hair stand on their neck, every player played their part today, and we will need the same energy, passion and commitment in the final against the favourites, Mountmear united.

Today's man of the match is Zak Brady, who just pipped Noah Rook. well done, Zak! Finn finishes speaking, all the team clap and cheer.

As they head off to the changing rooms.

"Don't forget training on tuesday evening" Coach Dempsey shouts!

Zak and Lee O'Brien, who are best friends, stroll back slowly to get changed and showered, when a voice shouts! "Well done, Zak" Great game!

Zak turns around and sees the boy with auburn hair waving to him, Zak waves back.

Who are you waving to? Lee asks. The boy with red hair, waving to me,

Zak replies. Look, he's just there in front of you.

Zak turns around, and the boy is gone, he was just there, did you not see him? yeah Zak, I think someone is losing their marbles!

Lee laughs and says, I'll race you back to the changing rooms.

Both the boys sprint to the changing rooms and reach there at the same time.

Zak looks over to the car park and sees

Coach Dempsey leave with his daughter,

Sarah Jessica. "She is the most beautiful girl that I ever seen"

Lee: she's well out of you're league, Brady!

"She has the deepest blue eyes" It's like looking at the ocean, Zak gushes.

She has eyes like the Pacific Ocean, deep blue eyes.

Jeez Brady, "You've got it bad", as i said, "she's out of your league", Lee teases. we'll see Lee, we'll see!

# CHAPTER 2
## *Best Friends*

The alarm goes off. it's 7.45 am, time to get up Zak, shouts his mum. You will be late for school.

It's Monday morning and it's a new week, she opens the blinds to let in the new day, the Moon is on it's way down, and the sun is on it's way up, what a beautiful morning, chirps Molly.

Molly is a very energetic woman, she has run 4 marathons, hundreds of half marathons, done thousands of keep-fit classes and walks 5 miles every day, she's been up since 5 am, and when she gets Zak to school, she'll stick on her headphones, listen to a podcast and walk the 5 miles briskly around the seashore, then she'll visit her parents Brian and Mary who are both retired and have a cup of coffee with them.

Zak gets up, brushes his teeth, and heads for the shower.

His Mum has breakfast ready and as an only child, Zak is somewhat spoiled, and mum molly has everything done for him, Zak wants to do things for himself, but his Mum fusses too much, Zak's Dad, Roy, sits down to eat his breakfast, a bowl of hot porridge with a few blueberries, a hot mug of coffee and 2 slices of toast with marmalade (thick cut).

Roy is 41 and is manager of the largest kitchen and bedding factory in Mountmear, the next largest town to Oakheart, he's been there for 18 years and finally got promoted to manager last Christmas.

Roy is a happy and very bubbly character who always wears a smile on his face.

He's been married to Molly for 15 years, plays some golf and is a big supporter of Arsenal football club, Zak had no choice but to follow in his Dad's footsteps and support the Gunners, too.

The doorbell rang, and Molly opened it to see Lee O'Brien standing on the doorstep, Is Zak ready yet? no, said Molly, come on in, he's just having breakfast, did you eat? are you hungry? asks Molly.

I have, but I could chance a slice of toast, Lee said as he smiles at Zak's Dad, come in and sit down Lee, I'll stick on the toast for you, said Roy.

Lee and Zak have been friends since primary school, everything they do, It's always together, It's the brother that Zak never had, and for Lee, he can chat and hang out with someone that understands him and can relate too. Lee has 3 sisters, they have no time for him or his undying love for Manchester united.

Lee is 6'1 and is very well built for a boy that just turned 15, he is naturally strong and his teammates have nicknamed him the brick, no one can get past him on the pitch, and they bounce off him if they try.

The boys are nearly at the end of their second year at Mountmear college, which is 4 miles from Oakheart, they get the bus at 8.30 and start school at 9. Zak and Lee are both loving second year at  Mountmear college but Zak has a dislike for one of the teachers, Ms. Stapleton.

She teaches maths, english and biology, Zak has her for all 3, just english for Lee.

Ms. Stapleton dislikes football and is always scolding Zak as he talks non-stop with his friends about it.

Zak hates biology and is falling behind the others.

Ms. Stapleton doesn't have time to teach classmates one-on- one and she expects everyone to study and perform equally well in class, Zak can't wait to hear the class bell so he can get to the next class, which is French.

There is a girl he likes in that class and he can't wait to see her, her name is Sarah Jessica, she is 5 foot 7, blonde hair with blue eyes that paralyse you when you look into them, the bell rings, and Zak is first up off the chair, he's glad to get out and away from the dead frogs and mice that are in glass containers on the shelves.

Zak enters the classroom.

Mr. Wright, the french teacher, is sitting at his desk, his long legs dangling in the air, he never sits in his chair, he's always sit's on the desk or on the big wooden radiator cover at the back of the class.

He glances at the clock on the wall, 3.20 pm, it's the last class of the day, nearly hometime, okay class, please be seated and open up your book, the french experience 1, turn to page 182 and Sarah Jessica, please start reading from the top, Mr. Wright walks around the class listening to Sarah Jessica read aloud.

Zak leans over his desk, arms folded and his chin lying on his arms, he gazes at Sarah Jessica as she reads the next paragraph, he is smitten with this little blonde girl, and lee knows it as he throws a crunched-up paper ball at Zak,

Wake up lover boy, you are drooling all over your desk, we'll need to bring in the mop, Lee said in a joking manner.

The class finishes, and the two boys make their way to the door, Lee teases Zak about Sarah Jessica again.

Why don't you go over and ask her out, no way said Zak as he tried to exit the classroom in a hurry.

Do you want me to ask her for you? laughs Lee, I'm away to get the bus, said Zak.

His face is blushing from embarrassment.

The boys board the bus, and Lee asks Zak what he's doing tonight, I'm going to play the new football game 'strikers" said Zak, Do you want to come over tonight? yeah, that would be great, I'll get my homework done and call over around seven, Lee answered.

The bus pulls up at it's stop in Oakheart and the boys get off, I'll see you later, said Zak as Lee walks up the hill to his house. Kicking stones all the way up.

# CHAPTER 3
## *Jack O'leary*

Zak is sitting on his bed playing the new football game strikers "on his game console wega 4000, that he got for christmas, he is waiting for his best friend Lee to join him as there is an option to play together in a team that takes on the best in europe.

A knock on the door makes Zak jump up and shout "It's for me", he opens his bedroom door, runs down the stairs and lets Lee into the house.

The game is set up for two players, and we're playing together in the one team said Zak exactly.

I hope you picked manchester united this time, said Lee.

I'm at home so it's arsenal tonight, Zak said with a huge grin on his face, Lee gave out a loud sigh and followed Zak upstairs to take on the cream of Europe.

Arsenal are beating Real Madrid 3-1 with 10 minutes left when Zak asks Lee, did he see the boy today, with auburn hair, watching the match? no, said Lee, I didn't see him, why do you keep asking? I have seen him a few times, and I can hear him shouting messages to me. Zak says, what? What does he say? Lee asked, he tells me to get into the box and stand on the penalty spot, things like that said Zak.

Did that big donkey defender from Rovers bang your head the other day in the semi-final, laughed Lee.

I can see him as clear as day, said Zak. he has auburn hair, blue eyes, he looks the same age as us and he is around 5 foot 8, Jeez, Zak, that's some description.

Maybe he's a rival player, and he is just spying on us to get as much information for the final, I heard the Mountmear boys are as competitive as heck, we will have our work cut out to beat them.

Maybe we will need your new friend to help us, Lee is laughing loudly and is making fun of Zak.

"I don't know who this boy is, but I know he's real, and he's helping me and I'm going to find out who he is and why is he helping me", Zak said in an angry tone.

Calm down Zak, I'm only teasing you.

Jeez, I didn't know you were so serious. Lee said in an apologetic mumble.

Aw, come on, Lee, Real Madrid just scored in the 89th minute.

Let's get through to the next round, we will be playing juventus and I want to go as far as possible in this tournament, said Zak.

Get in! Lee just scores and makes it 4-2, that's why I'm in the team, I'm the main man, I'm the main man, Lee starts singing to himself.

No Lee, Thierry Henry is the main man, not you, Thierry, Thierry, chants Zak.

Do you know, who would know, who that boy is? asks Lee, no, who, asked Zak our manager, Justin Dempsey, he knows everyone, ask him tomorrow at training.

I bet you he's a player from Mountmear, sent over to spy on us, they will do anything to win, they are so competitive said Lee.

The boys get to the final and play bayern munich, their hands are sore as bayern is playing a quick passing game.

Half time comes and the boys are relieved to get a break, right Lee! time to put bayern to the sword. I'm bringing on Wrighty for Freddie.

Do you think that's wise, Zak? it's very attacking.

It is Lee, that's the way I like to play! the boys can't score a goal and it goes to extra time, the game finishes 0-0 and it's penalties.

Lee and Zak's hands are numb, and they look forward to the dreaded penalty shootout.

Eight penalties are taken, and bergkamp steps up to take the fifth, he shoots and hits the post, ahhh, Zak, what are you doing? It's not me, it's the computer.

Yeah, yeah, lame excuse, Zak.

Ok big man, you have to save this, It's in your hands, Lee.

Well, It's in seaman's hands, actually, laughs Zak.

Muller strikes, and the keeper gets a hand on the ball but can't stop it from crossing the line.

Zak and Lee can't believe their eyes, they lost the final to bayern munich.

Aaagggggghhhhhhhhhh, the boys let a roar out of them that brings Molly bursting into the room, What's going on? Molly shouts.

Sorry, mrs brady, we lost and we're a bit annoyed.

Annoyed? Granny Brady can hear you both, and she lives two miles away.

Zak, it's bedtime. wrap this up now.

Ok, mum, we'll put the game away, Lee says his goodbyes and closes the front door.

Zak says goodnight to his Mum and Dad and closes his bedroom door.

The next day after school all the boys from the football team are asked to gather in the school hall, their manager Justin Dempsey is giving them a team talk before the final which is in two days.

He is going over tactics, defensive and attacking options, he is leaving no stone unturned and is making the team aware of Mountmears strengths and weaknesses.

He is making his team aware of their strengths too.

After the hour-long talk, Zak is walking to the training pitch behind the others and is hanging back for Coach Dempsey, excuse me, sir, can I have a word with you? certainly, Zak, says Coach Dempsey.

This might sound a bit strange, coach, but I have to ask: who is the boy that stands on the touchline and gives me advice every game? Is he from Mountmear? Is he local? Have you seen him before? slow down, boy, one question at a time.

I haven't seen any boy on the touchline, in any of our games.

Are you mistaking this boy as one of the subs from the other team? coach dempsey quips, no!!!! Zak bites back.

I have seen him with my own eyes at numerous games, and he's not a sub from the other team, he speaks to me and gives me advice on where I should be on the pitch, he even tells me to be in certain places before the ball is played, I keep thinking he's from the future.

Coach Dempsey lets out a loud sigh and tells Zak he will keep an eye out for the next game, maybe this fella is a ghost, has he got a name? I'll tell you what, Why don't you go down to the local library and dig up anything you can on mysterious boy/footballer from Oakheart.

Maybe you will find what you are looking for in there because I don't have a clue who he is, says Coach Dempsey.

Straight after training, Zak rushes down to the library and switches on the computer, he has to ask the libarian to switch on the microfiche player as he wants to read old newspaper articles.

Zak hasn't been in the library since he got his card when he first joined five years ago.

After scrolling for ages, Zak somehow stumbled on an article over sixty years ago, where the headline read, "talented young footballer dies in mysterious circumstances" Zak can't believe his eyes as he is gripped by the sad story of local boy Jack O'Leary, which takes up three pages in the local paper at the time "Oakheart news " Zak keeps scrolling through the archives and sees more articles on Jack O'Leary, "Gifted young football star gone too soon" "Young football magician dies tragically " "Community rocked by young footballers' death "

Zak gets a few copies made and is in a hurry to get home and let his best friend lee know what he found at the library.

Zak is happy and sad at the same time. he starts questioning himself as he walks home.

Is this the boy on the touchline?

Is he really a ghost? a phantom? An apparition?

Is he going to be my friend?

A foe? a spectre?

Will my friends think I'm going slightly mad?

Zak gets inside the door of his house and makes his way into the living room, he wants to phone Lee and tell him what he has discovered, mum, can I use the phone? I want to ring Lee, I need to ring Lee!

I'm on the phone with your aunt Majella, she's ringing me from Australia, I'll be another ten minutes at least, What's the matter, son? It's ok mum, I'll call over and see Lee now, Zak said as he walked out the front door and made his way to Lee's house.

Ding-dong goes the doorbell the door opens, hello Mrs O'Brien hello Zak is Lee there?

Yes, he is in the garden with his Dad can I go and see him of course, Zak, come on in Zak goes out to the garden and sees his best friend Lee weeding the garden with his Dad. Can I help?

Asks Zak you sure can said Lee's dad just grab a spade and help Lee dig up the weeds by the garden shed.

Ok, Mr. O'Brien, sure thing, Zak tells Lee what he found out in the library.

Lee can't believe What he's hearing that's unbelievable, Zak. unreal Do you think he's the mystery boy at the matches?

I don't know Lee, I have to find out more about Jack O'leary I am very intrigued now.

It said this boy died 60 years ago.

He must have relatives somewhere in Mountmear or even here in Oakheart?

What if he's related to you, Zak? Lee asks.

I'm gonna ask Dad when he comes home from work.

Someone must know his story.

How many times has this boy appeared to you? Lee asks, just a few but I'm sure it won't be the last time I see him.

So, he is 5 foot 8 with auburn hair, has freckles and has appeared twice to you? Lee asks.

Yeah, that's him. have you seen him?

How many times do I have to tell you no?

I haven't seen him.

Do you know what, Lee?

You haven't seen him yet! but you will, I'm sure of it!

Do you know what, Lee?

Nothing really happens in Oakheart, but I believe something special is going to happen, mark my words, Lee, something's going to happen.yeah, yeah, Zak. dream on. too much chat from you boys, these weeds won't dig themselves, Lee's Dad, jokes.

CHAPTER 4
Sarah Jessica / Cup Final

It's Saturday It's Cup Final day Zak wakes up at 8 and springs out of bed Where are my boots? Where's my boots? Zak's Dad rushes into the room, What's up, son? What's all the commotion about? my boots, dad? I can't find my boots and It's cup final day.

They are down in the kitchen, son I gave them a good clean and polish last night, they are ready and all spruced up, like brand-new thanks, dad, you shouldn't have gone to any trouble no trouble, son, no trouble at all.

The doorbell rings twice, and Molly Brady opens the door good morning Lee How are you? I'm excited, really excited, said Lee. is Zak up yet? yes, he's up and ready to go, replied Molly.

Goodbye mum. see you later and wish us luck today, Zak said.

As he skipped past his mum at the dorway, best of luck, son, but you won't need it, your Dad and I will be there to cheer you on.

What time is the bus? Zak! Zak!

What time is the bus?

Zak doesn't hear his dad call out, Roy Brady closes the front door.

He didn't hear me, molly, he sprinted down the lane and never heard me.

It's ok, Roy, sure, we'll see him at the game later. (Molly didn't always have the answers but she was nearly always right) the bus pulls up at the school the excitement was unreal.

The atmosphere was building for weeks and finally, the day had come, it was cup final day. coach dempsey has now made his final call for everyone to get on the bus.

All the boys hurry to get on Finn and noah grab the backseat Lee and Zak are the last to get on.

As Zak is climbing the steps on the bus, a voice calls out! good luck today, Zak! it was Sarah Jessica, Coach Dempsey's daughter.

Zak's face turns Bright Red, and he tries to respond to Sarah Jessica: but his words come out wrong and he mumbles something that even he doesn't understand. What was that?

Sarah Jessica said oh nothing! Zak said with an embarrassed frown.

# The Ghost of Zak Brady

I want to ask you something Sarah Jessica.

What is it? asks Sarah Jessica, Do you want to go to the cinema this friday night? wow! that is a very brave thing of you to ask, says Sarah Jessica.

Is that a no, then? Zak asks apologically.

No, it's a yes! I would love to go to the cinema with you, I'm a big fan of the popcorn jokes, Sarah Jessica.

I'll pick you up at 7:30. Zak said in an excited tone.

Sure, I'll see you then, Zak. play well today, play well.

Sarah Jessica's words was the perfect start to Zak's day.

Zak Can't believe she said yes, he immediately starts to daydream about her, he sits in his seat and smiles the whole way to the stadium. The bus pulls up to the stadium, It's an old ground which is over 50 years old.

The roof needs to be replaced as it leaks on the west side when it rains heavily.

Last year's final between Mountmear united and Sliabh Rua saw fans rushing to get cover as the roof leaked in the heavy rain, that battered the old stadium for hours. some of the fans were entering the pitch to get away from the heavy rain was falling hard, and the committee didn't want a repeat of that happening this year, they are hoping for better weather.

They have checked the weather and it's going to be mild, with a little breeze, so ideal conditions for the school final. 16 school teams from 4 regions compete for the enda tolley memorial trophy, enda tolley was the man who created the first schools Football League and cup over 50 years ago and encouraged schools from the 4 regions to partake in this new adventure. enda passed away 2 years ago due to poor health and was made honorary president of the schools just before he took ill, photos of enda are plastered inside the Stadium, smiling from ear to ear, one of the jolliest men you could have ever met, he always had time for people and always had an encouraging word for every boy that kicked a ball for any of the school teams.

His family are sitting in the main stand and will be presenting the trophy to the winning team today.

Enda is sorely missed and is always talked about whenever a match is played, he was a fine footballer in his day,a creative midfielder and always had an eye for goal, he had trials for liverpool, Celtic and newcastle but was always carrying an injury and didn't make the grade.

The team get off the bus and takes a look at the pitch. mountmear united are already on the pitch, wearing black training tops doing drills, shooting practice and gentle stretches.

Right lads! let's get changed and get out onto this pitch.

Get your legs warmed up!! shouts Coach Dempsey.

All the boys have changed into their home strip, red and white hoops and enter the pitch to the north bank side.

Zak looks up, and the first person who catches his eye is Sarah Jessica, her blue eyes sparkle in the afternoon sun and in an instant,

Zak's face lights up, and his broad smile is easily recognized by the whole team.

The other boys start to tease Zak about Sarah Jessica and start to sing to Zak, you love sj, she loves you, you love SJ, she loves you, Zak is mortified, and his face is bright red, and he is trying to stop the other boys from teasing but they ignore him and keep singing louder.

Sarah Jessica is smiling very softly but her mum, Ingrid, has a stern look on her face and is staring very hard at Bobby Kelly and Gary Rice, who continued to sing on their own.

They suddenly realise that the woman who is staring at them is Sarah Jessica's Mum, she is originally from sweden and also has blonde hair and blue eyes.

Both defenders wave and softly say sorry in the direction of ingrid dempsey, she has an icy stare that would cut you in half, she was known as a frosty character and a woman you wouldn't get on the wrong side of.

The referee blew his whistle and told both teams that the game will start in 5 minutes, Coach Dempsey has signalled his team to the touchline, everyone is in a huddle, and Justin Dempsey gives a sharp and short speech to the boys: let's play to our strengths, be positive, attack together, and defend together but most importantly play with freedom and smile, let's enjoy this cup final.

Finn rook takes over and he rallies the team, let's get stuck in from the start, don't give the ball away and keep moving all over the pitch, let's bring the cup back to Oakheart.

The referee blows his whistle, and the cup final is underway, the ball is moved forward quickly from mountmear, and they waste no time in getting the first shot on target, Oakheart's keeper gets down well to his left and holds on tight to the ball, that will give him some confidence going forward.

The match is evenly matched, and both teams are finding chances hard to come by, Zak had a couple of chances to pass or shoot but took too long on the ball and possession was lost, he's not himself, and he is steadily looking over at Sarah Jessica.

Finn has noticed and calls over to Zak. hey Brady, keep your mind and focus on the game and not the girl. Zak pretends not to hear him and trudges over the halfway line.

Just before half time, Mountmear get a direct freekick on the edge of the box when a clumsy foul by Lee has maybe given Mountmear a good chance to take the lead at the end of the half.

Two mountmear players are beside the ball, the number 8 steps over the ball and the number 10 hits it, left-footed and smashes it off the bar and the right back from Oakheart clears the ball into the crowd.

Oakheart's number 9 is standing on the halfway line, shouting for his team to get up the pitch, Mountmear have all the possession and are putting the pressure on this Oakheart team. corner after corner comes in on top of the Oakheart defence but they defend robustly, and the halftime whistle is blown and Oakheart is relieved to get off the pitch 0-0. the boys all sit down in the changing room, the room is dark and mouldy, and the dampness is easy to see in the corners of this old musty room.

Justin dempsey walks in and straight away starts shouting, what is happening out there?

You are all over the place!!, midfield!! I don't see you at all, not one of you have turned up, Brady!

What's up with you today? You lose the ball every time, I do not see anything that will keep you on that pitch in the second half, wake up, son! are you daydreaming out there?

Lee, the brick, stands up and tries to stick up for Zak, it might be nerves, sir, I kinda felt nervous at the start, but maybe others still feel nervous. listen, O'Brien! I've managed enough times to know when nerves kick in, and I also know when players are thinking of other things when their minds should be on one thing, and that's football.

The coach is seething and stares directly at Zak! Brady !!!, not my daughter, get your act together or you'll be sitting in the stands with her in the second half, coach dempsey leaves the changing rooms, kicking a bottle of water on the way out.

Finn speaks to the team, Jeez, I've never seen the coach so mad, Zak, you need to do something out there.

He must have seen you constantly staring at his daughter, Zak again is embarrassed and tries to change the subject but David Ryan and aidan wilson are in his ear over the managers daughter.

You love her, you love her, Zak gets up and throws a boot at them, shut up, shut up you silly ejits, Zak walks out, his face a picture of thunder, he is ready to explode, and his best friend Lee puts an arm around him and they both walk out.

Zak, you have to do something in this second half. You're not going to get into coach dempsey's good books if you don't buck up, stop looking at Sarah Jessica, focus on your game, you can do some magic out there.

I don't know what's happening, I can't concentrate or focus on the game, all I see is her blue eyes, blonde hair and charming smile.

Zak replied. I don't see that boy on the touchline today either, I thought he was going to help me today. Jeez Zak, you have the talent, It's got nothing to do with that boy on the sideline, there Isn't even a boy on the sidelines, It's in your imagination. he's real! he's a ghost, he exists, I have seen him numerous times, I thought you believed me Lee? some friend you are! aw, come on, Zak.

I believe in you and your ability as a footballer you can't rely on this phantom boy.

I don't want to talk about him again Lee, let's play football.

Zak walks onto the pitch and starts to talk to himself, Where are you? Why haven't you turned up today?

I really need you!! the second half kicks off, and its all mountmear for the first 10 minutes, Zak looks up, and he sees Coach Dempsey getting Paul Tierney warmed up, he plays in my position, Zak whispers to himself, I'll show him.

The ball is kicked up to Celtic's forward, and he looks for Zak to lay it off, Oakheart is starting to get a grip in midfield now.

Finn, David Ryan and Zak are making sharp crisp passes to each other and Mountmear can't get near them, Zak spots noah on the right-hand side of the pitch and sprays a 30 yard pass right to his feet, noah takes on the defender on the outside and goes past him with ease, Coach Dempsey is shouting instructions from the byeline, get up the field, get in the box, get in the box. 5 players from oakheart sprint forward, suddenly, Zak hears a voice in his ear, It's very wispy, an eerie feeling comes over Zak as he looks up to see that boy standing beside Coach Dempsey, the voice comes again," stand on the edge of the 18 yard box, right in the middle and wait". the box is very crowded with attackers from Oakheart and defenders from Mountmear.

Zak hangs back and hovers around the edge of the box, staying very central, the ball comes in and is headed back out to Noah.

He drops the shoulder, beats his man and whips in the cross, sailing over the defender's heads.

The ball has so much pace on it, it clears the big Mountmear number 6 and is struck first time by Zak,

Who strikes it cleanly on the instep, and the ball hits the underside of the bar and bounces down over the line, the keeper hasn't moved due to the ferocious impact of the shot. the oakheart crowd erupt and jumps up and down in the stands, Sarah Jessica is waving and smiling at Zak, Coach Dempsey is still shouting to his players, focus, focus, stay alert.

Mountmear move the ball quickly and switch the ball out to the left-wing, their number 11 is quick and very tricky, he knocks the ball past the outstretched leg of the right-back and goes to cross the ball on his left foot, Bobby Kelly, the butcher's son, goes to close him down, but the tricky winger feints the cross and takes the ball onto his right foot and curls the ball from 22 yards into the top corner. The keeper gets his fingers to it but can't prevent it from hitting the top corner of the net, the sides are level, and Oakheart concede straight from the kickoff.

Coach Dempsey is furious, and it's Mountmear united the favourites who celebrate and cheer. both teams make changes, the game is stifled, and it is nearing full-time, penalties are looming, and it's anyone's guess who will win this cup final? There is nothing to separate these two teams, and a draw would be a fair result, but it has to go to penalties, no extra time, no replays, it has to be settled today.

Celtic's striker goes down off the ball and is in a lot of pain and can't continue, Coach Dempsey sends on Ronan Powell for the last 3 minutes and tells him to make a nuisance of himself. the free kick is 35 yards out and is on the left-hand side of the pitch,

Ronan puts the ball down and asks the referee is it indirect or direct? the referee says it's indirect, Powell speaks to Finn, who gently pushes the sub away from the ball, Finn whispers to Zak, and they get into a huddle between themselves.

Suddenly, Zak hears the voice again, walk to the left-hand side of the wall, wait for the ball to come and let it roll past you and cut in past the incoming defender, dummy the next defender and shoot low to the left of the keeper.

Finn is looking at the back post and signals to his big men to gather around the back.

The 6-yard box is chockablock with eighteen players tussling for space. The Mountmear team have everybody back and are trying to defend this free kick, they seem to think the ball is going deep to the back post, the whistle blows, and Finn disguises the pass and slides the ball to Zak, he lets the ball roll past him.

The voice comes again, cut in past the incoming defender, the defender comes across and slides in, Zak cuts back in and avoids the challenge, the next defender comes flying across, and Zak pretends to shoot, the defender tries to block the shot and sticks a leg out.

Zak doesn't shoot, he hears the voice, shoot hard low to the left! shoot hard low to the left Zak hits it hard and aims for the bottom corner, the ball whistles towards the left-hand post, the keeper is wrong-footed and goes the opposite way.

The ball hits the post and spins across the goal line, the keeper tries to react, but the pace of the ball has him beat the spin on the ball takes it over the line, and it ends up nestling in the right-hand corner of the net.

Oakheart Celtic have struck in the 89th minute, the crowd cheers, and an almighty roar comes from the dugout, Dempsey's men have the advantage in the dying moments.

Mountmear, get on with it and hit it long up the pitch. It's desperate measures now for the favourites and they are looking to level up this match. they force a corner, the referee looks at his watch, this must be the last chance for Mountmear, 16 times winners of this cup, the most that any school has won it. The corner comes in and is headed back out for another one, It's taken again, and this time it's flicked on at the near post. Zak hears the voice again, stand at the back post and don't move the ball is flicked on and the number 10, Mountmear's top goalscorer in the league and cup gets a powerful head on it and directs it to the back post, it is rocketing towards goal and the keeper is beat but Zak is standing at the back post and heads it way to safety.

The whistle blows, and It's all over, Oakheart Celtic win the cup for the 7th time all the oakheart team rush to Zak and hug him, he stood out in the second half and won that final with 2 goals and a last-minute clearance.

Every player lifts Zak onto their shoulders and walks around the pitch chanting his name, Zak Brady, Zak Brady, man of the match.

Zak looks over, and the young boy is standing on the touchline smiling, he turns and walks way, he disappears into the crowd.

Wait, wait, shouts Zak, running across to the dugout. coach dempsey meets Zak and wraps his arms around him, I knew you would come, good son, well done, well done.

Sarah Jessica appears in front of Zak, well, played Zak, great game as she smiles with her blue eyes. Thanks. Sarah Jessica, thanks!

Sarah Jessica kisses Zak on the cheek and says I'll see you later.

Zak's face goes bright red, but he doesn't care, he has Sarah Jessica's heart and she has his.

The trophy is being carried onto the field by the tolley family and Mountmear have already received their runners-up medals, the Oakheart boys are dancing and singing in their traditional red and white hoops strip.

They go up to lift the cup and rejoice in the moment they have been dreaming all year.

Finn holds the enda tolley memorial trophy up high and is roaring Oakheart, Oakheart, all the team join in and Chant Oakheart's name into the early evening.

# CHAPTER 5
## *Leukemia*

Sunday Morning, the day after the Cup Final, Zak's mum enters the bedroom and opens the curtains, breakfast is ready, son. time to wake up; Lee is on his way over.

What time is it, Mum? it's 9.30 Zak, time to get up and get your breakfast.

What time did you say Lee was coming over? he's on his way, son; he'll be here any moment now. Zak jumps out of his bed, goes in to the bathroom, brushes his teeth and runs downstairs, singing Oakheart, Oakheart, we are the champions.

The doorbell rings Molly opens the door come in Lee, he's just eating his breakfast.

Lee walks into the kitchen, Zak is eating a slice of toast and a boiled egg.

Hey Zak, how is it going? all good Lee, it was a great day yesterday, Zak breaks into a song we are the champions, we are the champions both boys sing and Roy, Zak's dad walks in What's with all the screeching? i thought there was a couple of cats in here, Roy starts to smirk, and then a big smile comes across his face I'm only joking, boys, sing up, you guys were brilliant yesterday.

The phone rings, and Molly answers it, hello, Molly Brady.

Here, who's this? I see, oh thanks for letting me know Molly puts the phone down, Zak, can I have a word with you? sure mum what's up? that was miss stapleton, your biology teacher What? your teacher What did she want? She said Sarah Jessica was taken to the hospital an hour ago the ambulance was at their house for a couple of hours What happened, SJ? Zak asks.

She wasn't feeling very well last night and was very weak she had a fever and recurrent nosebleeds.

Zak's heart dropped will she be alright, mum? I'm sure she will be ok, son she is in good hands now at the hospital Zak walks into the living room, and the tears start to flow he tries to cover up his eyes with his forearm as Lee enters the room. is everything alright, Zak? What happened to Sarah Jessica? Do you want to go and see her in hospital? I just want to be left alone, if you don't mind, Lee! she was looking great yesterday at the game, How could she be in hospital today? I think I'll go on my bike and call in and see her for 5 minutes. I'll go with you Zak, if you don't mind!

Thanks Lee, we'll go and get her something in the shop, I'll ask my Dad for a few euros. Zak gets money from his Dad and both boys leave for the hospital.

Zak and Lee enter the hospital, they walk over to the reception desk, hello, we're here to see Sarah Jessica Dempsey, please, one moment, the recepionist says. she is on floor 3.

Room 217 you have only 45 minutes left of visiting time. thank you, miss, the boys rush to the lift, hit that button, lee, button 3.

Lee pushes the button for floor 3, the lift door closes and in no time reopens on the third floor. Room 215,216, here we are Lee, room 217. as Zak enters the room, he see's Coach Dempsey with his wife, and they are both crouching over the bed, Zak knocks on the door, hello? can I come in?

Mr. and Mrs. Dempsey turn around, they look like they have been crying for ages, is Sarah Jessica going to be ok? Coach Dempsey walks over to Zak.

I'm afraid to say, our little Sarah Jessica has leukaemia, she had it for the past 9 years and the haemato oncologists have said, that she has lasted way beyond what normal cancer paitents last.

I don't understand, coach. she always looks fine!

I never knew she was sick. aww son, she didn't want anyone to know or worry about her. she kept everything private.

She was in a lot of pain and was getting treatment for years.

Between the hospital and home, that is where Sarah spent most of her time.

"If you don't mind, Zak, we would like to be alone with our daughter". yeah, sure coach, I must be on my way home anyway.

Zak stops at the door, he turns around and walks over to the bed, Where he sees all these leads and wires hooked up to Sarah Jessica. the tears trickle down his face, I don't want sj to die I love her.

I love her, coach. Mrs. Dempsey puts her arm around Zak, pulls him in and gives him a big hug, we don't want her to die either.

The Dempsey's sob and hug Zak tightly, they spend the next while just hugging and crying.

Lee looks on from the doorway and he even has a tear in his eye.

Zak eventually leaves the hospital with Lee and tells him that he has this horrible pain in his heart. That's your heart breaking Zak.

How do you know that, Lee? I saw it in a movie once.

You'll be ok in a couple of years. a couple of years! I want to be ok now, not in a couple of years.

Zak looks dumbfounded, he doesn't understand what's happening, he rubs his eyes again, he doesn't want to let his best friend catch him crying, again.

The boys cycle for home talking about love, heartbreak and death! Zak parks his bike at the side of the house and turns his key in the door, his Mum is standing, waiting for him, she opens her arms and gives him a big hug, everything will be ok, son, she's in the best place now and will get the treatment she needs to get better.

Zak embraces his mum, and the tears start to flow.

We were supposed to go on our first date this friday night! stupid, stupid leukemia!! it's going to be ok, son, that young lady, Sarah Jessica she's one tough cookie.

You will have plenty of dates at the cinema with Sarah Jessica in the future.

Zak gives his mum a kiss on the cheek and says he's going to bed.

Goodnight son, tomorrow is a brand-new day, new day, new possibilities.

Goodnight mum, (Zak trudges upstairs to his room; it's been a long day)

# CHAPTER 6
## *Ms. Stapleton*

The school bell rings, and that's the noise that some students dread on a Monday morning. Had they their homework done? did they study enough? had they the correct books for today's classes? Zak, Lee, Finn and noah were standing by the noticeboard in the school corridor when Ms. Stapleton walked past, she stopped, turned around and said in a very high pitch tone, the bell has rung, and 4 of my students are loitering in the hall. Come along, boys, you're already one minute late for class.

Lee moves first and shuffles his way into class, followed by Noah and Finn.

Will you not be attending today's class, master Brady? before Zak could answer, he felt a sharp pain in his ear as Ms. Stapleton was pulling him into her class by his ear.

Ahhhh, what did you do that for? you are late for class and I don't like boys hanging about outside when they should be in class, and especially in my class, now take a seat and get your books out! Zak isn't impressed with Ms. Stapleton, she is probably his least favourite teacher, Zak took a dislike to her when he got detention for the one and only time. He was kicking a ball up against the wall when Ms. Stapleton confiscated his football, on his first day at Oakheart College.

Before Zak took his seat, he asked Ms. Stapleton, why are you so mean? and when am I getting my ball back? Ms. Stapleton shouted at Zak, sit down or it will be detention again, don't push me, boy, I'm not in the mood for you today! Zak sits down and slams his bag on the table, he looks over at lee and mumbles something, What? Lee asked I didn't say anything.

I heard you say something, Zak, Ms. Stapleton is directly staring at Zak. I'll tell you later, Ms. Staplewitch is watching me ... the bell rings and Zak bounces up from his seat, don't forget to revise pages 79 to 85 as you will have an exam next week.

As Lee and Zak leave the classroom, Ms. Stapleton calls Zak back and asks to have a quiet word with him, alone. What do you want, miss?

Zak, I know it's a difficult time for you as I believe you and Sarah Jessica are very close.

You don't know what you're talking about, miss! it's ok Zak, I understand that this is hard to take in and it seems so cruel. A young girl plagued with cancer and her whole life ahead of her.

I just want to tell you of my own sister, she died really young and we were all devastated. Jenny was 17 when she lost her life.

She had osteosarcoma, a type of bone cancer.

She only found out on her 16th birthday that she had that dreadful cancer. We were a small family but we were all very close.

My mum and Dad never got over her death and they passed away a few years back, they died within 12 weeks of each other.

That cancer didn't just kill our Jennifer, it killed our family too. I just wanted to say Zak, if you ever need anything or if you want to talk to anyone, then i'm always here for you, the Dempsey's will need you and as many as their friends now and over the next few months.

I can arrange for a counsellor to call into class some day, get you and your friends ready for…. for what? shouts Zak, her death? Sarah Jessica dying? I don't want to talk about it, leave me alone! I hate you!! I hate you!!

Zak storms out of the class, he is very upset, he pushes the double doors to go outside, and as he enters the playground, he breaks down and cries,

He lets all of his frustrations and anger out as he drops to his knees, why? why her? why SJ? please god, not her!!! all of the football team gather around Zak in a circle, they are shielding him from the rest of the school.

Lee bends down on one knee and puts his arm around Zak.

Come on Zak, let's get out of here, let's go to the park.

Zak gets up and leaves with Lee, as both boys leave the playground, Ms. Stapleton is standing by the basketball court, she was watching everything unfold for Zak. Mr. Wright, the French teacher, joins Ms. Stapleton, It's good that the boys have a match tomorrow, anything to get Zak's mind on something else, I agree, Mr. Wright,  Zak is not in a good place at the moment, this game might have come at a good time for him and the team.

Both teachers continue to talk and walk together towards the staff room. They are both really concerned about Zak.

The school bell rings aloud, and that signals lunch is over, and the next class is ready to begin.

Mr. Wright is putting up the team sheet on the notice board, most of the boys gather round him, the team is unchanged from the cup final.

Mr. Wright will be taking the league match instead of Coach Dempsey. He was a former youth player for auxerre, his claim to fame was when he played in a pre-season game with Rick Cantona, liam blanc and virgil cisse in the late 80s.

The visiting team to play Oakheart Celtic was scarton town, they currently lie 3rd in the league and are just 1 point behind the home team.

1. Mountmear 39
2. Oakheart Celtic 36
3. Scarton Town 35
4. Oakheart Rovers 33
5. Black Hawks 31
6. Sliabh Rua 28
7. Red Bears 28
8. Dun Mount 27

9.  Cadden City 27
10. Forest Celtic 24

Oakheart Celtic play their game in hand tomorrow against scarton town, 3 points behind mountmear at the halfway stage.

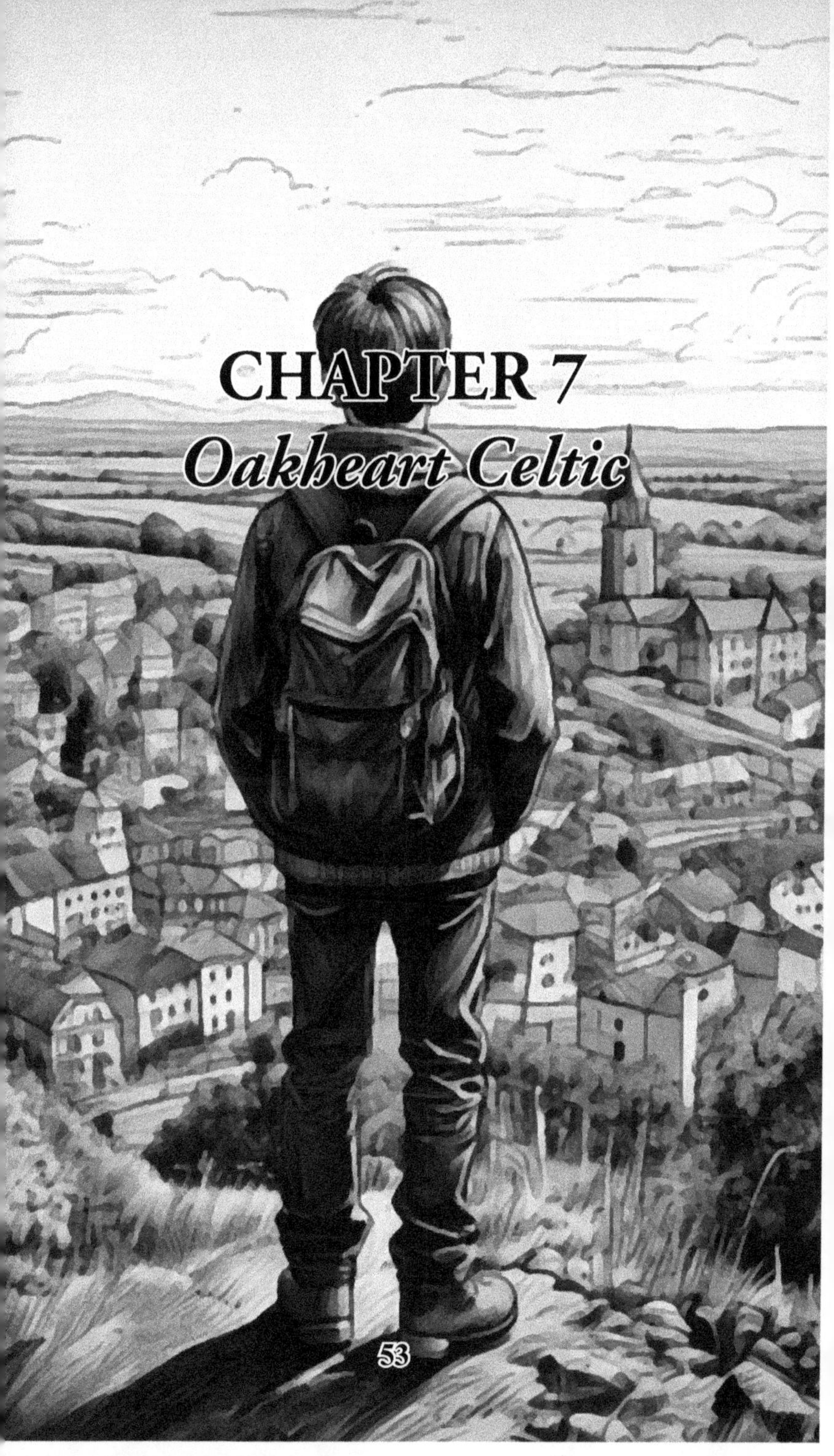
CHAPTER 7
Oakheart Celtic
53

It's a foggy tuesday evening at Oakheart and It's 2nd vs 3rd in the league.

Mr. Wright picks the team for the first time in the absence of Coach Dempsey who is away on compassionate leave. The game kicks off, and it's the away side that threaten first, with their top goalscorer Kieran Rack who narrowly shoots over from 18 yards. the yellow shirts and black hoops are swarming all over the Oakheart penalty box.

The referee blows the whistle and awards a penalty. the number 4 for the home side has his head in his hands, he has just brought down scarton town's tricky winger. Jorge Reyes, who is a Spanish exchange student from Sevilla.

Some of the Oakheart defence aren't happy with the Spanish Winger, they claim that Reyes took a dive over the butcher's Son leg, Bobby Kelly is still arguing with the referee and is duly booked, he will have to watch himself now, as there is still over an hour left of the game.

Kieran Rack walks to the penalty area and places the ball on the spot, oakheart's keeper is jumping over and back the goal line, trying to put scarton's top goal scorer off.

The whistle blows and the number 10 makes no mistake from the spot as he sends Celtic's keeper the wrong way. Oakheart are 1 nil down and face a massive task here to get back into this game.

Finn grabs the ball and calls his brother Noah over to the centre circle, Finn touches the ball to Noah, and he finds Zak

On the edge of the semi circle, Zak switches the play to the far side of the pitch and puts the ball right on the toe of the left Winger.

Zak is slowly making his way up the pitch when he hears a voice, follow David, follow David.

Zak changes his run and drifts over to the left-hand side of the pitch and goes behind David Ryan.

Again, the voice says in a whispering tone, follow David, follow David and shadow him. The Winger goes on a Mazy run, he takes on 1 defender, beats him and takes on another, he goes past him with ease, David Ryan is on the edge of the box and takes on another defender, he knocks it past him, he has a defender and the keeper to beat.

Zak hears the voice again, follow David, shadow him. David Ryan is just about to take on the last defender, when scarton's number 3 stretches out a leg and touches the ball to his right.

Zak, who was shadowing behind David, finds himself one on one with the keeper, the keeper comes rushing out, the voice whispers, wait until the keeper goes down and then chip it over him.

The keeper comes and dives at the feet of Zak and he listens to the voice. Just as the keeper thinks he has the ball in his grasp, Zak just dinks the ball over him.

The ball takes 2 bounces and rolls into the middle of the net, the Scarton defenders try in vain to stop the ball from crossing the line but just can't reach it in time.

Oakheart celtic level up the match and it's that man again, Zak Brady who is in the right place at the right time.

Oakheart's number 9 asks Zak, How did you know where the ball was gonna end up? you seem to be always on hand when the ball is loose in the box, It's my friend Jack o' Leary, he tells me where to go! Jack Who? The number 9 asked? that fella standing on the touchline, Zak points towards the touchline and Jack o'Leary is standing beside Mr. Wright, look, Tyrone, he's giving me the thumbs up, the forward looks across to the touchline.

I don't see anyone Zak, maybe you're seeing things? no, he's standing right beside our new coach and he's waving over to me. I think you have finally lost the plot, brady, there is no one beside our new coach. whatever! Zak said.

I can see him and that's all that matters to me! the referee is calling Zak and Tyrone to get back into their half as he wants to restart the game. 8 minutes remain of the first half and Mr. Wright is giving some instructions to Noah, the oldest of the twins.

Oakheart are making a sub and to Zak's amazement, Mr. Wright is holding up the number 6, It's Lee, Zak's best friend.

Zak throws his hands in the air and gives his new coach a puzzled look, it's more of shock really. Paul Tierney, the number 13, is coming on for only his 4th appearance.

He's a tough tackling, no nonsense midfielder who takes no prisoners, most of the team have been together for over 8 years and they know nearly everything about each other. They are a bunch of jokers and are always messing about.

The 2 goalkeepers who are the funniest, Luke Kennedy and Patrick Shaw have the rest of the team in stitches, every away game is a hoot. They are like a big family, with plenty of laughs and teasing one another constantly.

Coach Dempsey used to play defence vs attack regularly, and the defence have struck up a bond that is unbreakable, the attackers are the same, and they have great camaraderie and friendship within the squad. Coach Dempsey would always play 7 against 7, with himself and reserve goalkeeper Patrick Shaw being the referees.

Sometimes, it would get a little heated, but it always end with all 15 players laughing and joking.

Scarton town restart the game and their number 7 tries to thread a ball through both of Oakheart centre halves, Celtic's number 5 spots the pass early and moves across scarton's number 9.

He passes to his right back, who in turn finds the left back moving up to the halfway line. He keeps the ball moving and shouts rook!

Finn takes the pass on the outside of his right boot and knocks the ball past his marker, Noah is calling for the ball as he sprints down the right-hand side of the pitch. Finn looks up and slides the ball between three of the Scartons players,

Zak hears the voice again, move towards the near post, move to the near post, Zak jogs towards the scarton penalty area, Noah beats 2 players, but his pass is intercepted by scarton's number 8.

The Scarton midfielder starts a counterattack and is bursting through the Oakheart midfield, there is a sudden crashing noise as Oakheart's sub Paul Tierney smashes into the scarton midfielder, he wins the ball cleanly, but he follows through and knocks the number 8 flying, he looks up and hits a 20-yard pass high into the box, Tyrone Reilly jumps highest and gets the slightest touch on the ball, it's spinning towards goal and scarton's keeper (which, by the way, is being watched by a number of premier league scouts) get's an outstretched hand onto the ball and tips the ball on to the bar, the ball is coming back off the bar and 3 of scarton defenders are rushing back to clear the ball, but Zak hears the voice and steals into the near post to nod the ball over the body of the goalkeeper that's rooted to the ground.

It's 2-1 and the large crowd are celebrating and cheering, Zak looks around and is hoping that somehow Sarah Jessica is in the crowd, he scowers the people from top to bottom, but no sign of Sarah Jessica. he has a lump in his throat, he's happy he scored and the the team is winning, but it is sad that SJ Isn't here to see him.

The second half flies in, and the match finishes 2-1 to Oakheart. They go level at the top of the table with Mountmear and nearly on the same goal difference. What a team!

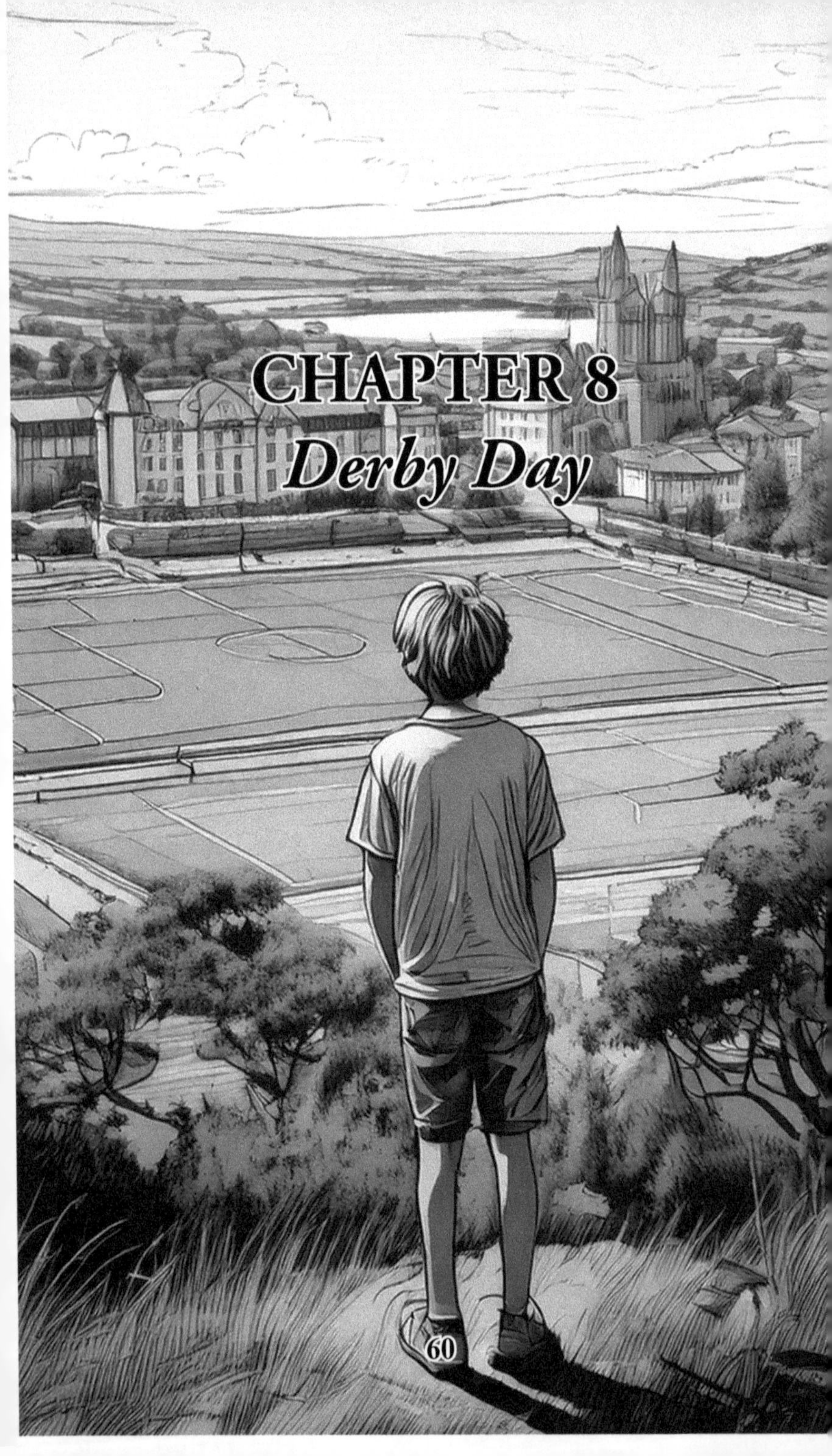

CHAPTER 8
Derby Day
60

The light was sneaking in through the side of the curtains, and the darkness was fading away over the snow-covered hills. It was saturday morning, early part of November, snow had fallen overnight, and the trees at the bottom of Zak's garden were covered from top to bottom. everything was white, rooftops, garden sheds, fields, even parts of the road were white. it was derby day, Oakheart Celtic vs Oakheart Rovers these games were always hard-fought and hard to call, you wouldn't want to call this game either way.

Zak could hear the phone ringing downstairs, his mum, Molly answers, and Zak can hear her say, yes, I'll tell him Mr Wright, have a good day.

Zak! his Mum shouts upstairs, the game is definitely on, be at the school by noon.

Zak bounces out of bed and gets into the shower, he dries himself off and then brushes his teeth, his mum has breakfast ready, and his sports bag is packed with his boots hanging out of it.

Zak was in a hurry, and he was shovelling down the crunchy nut wheat flakes like there was no tomorrow, you're going to give yourself indigestion, son! man dear, relax and enjoy your food, Molly then called roy for his breakfast, mum, I have to go soon, it's too early, Zak, you have plenty of time! I'm going over to Lee's house first, we will walk to the school, sure, your dad will take you both as he's going in town anyways to buy some paint for the living room.

It's ok, Mum, we will walk.

Zak finishes his breakfast, grabs his kit bag and leaves the house.

Zak is walking down the lane, kicking stones and visualising the net bulging, as he is getting closer to Lee's house, an ambulance speeds past with the sirens on, Zak looks back at the ambulance and whispers in to himself, whoever is inside, I hope you're alright. It was a common thing if you saw an ambulance, some people would bless themselves, others would look for a dog,

Zak always saw his Mum and Dad say a few words whenever an ambulance was near, superstition? most of his teammates were the same, aidan wilson, the left back, would always wear 2 pairs of socks for a match. he lost a match 6-0 wearing 1 pair of socks, so, from then on, he wore 2 pair for luck. Tyrone Reilly, the striker, would always come out last for any match, he couldn't come out early as he thought it was bad luck. David Ryan, the midfielder, would put his left sock on first if the team were at home, if the team was playing away from home, he would put his right sock on first.

Noah and Finn rook had exactly the same superstitions, both players would tie numerous knots in their laces and would always put their right boot on first. Lee O'Brien, midfielder and Zak's best friend would always kiss a ring, that his Grandmother gave him before she died.

He would kiss it six times as it was his lucky number, before removing the item before a game.

He said that he isn't superstitious at all but he feels this habit brings him Good Luck.

Zak arrives at Lee's house, rings the bell, the door opens, and Sophia welcomes Zak inside.

Lee! It's Zak here for you. lee has 3 sisters, Sophia, Marianne and Leanne. they are all older than Lee, they spoil him as he is the youngest and the only boy in the house.

Lee doesn't like too much fuss, his nickname at football is the brick, and sometimes at home with his sisters, he tends to act like a brick.

Zak is an only child, and he is fascinated with the 3 Sisters, Jeez Lee, I would love to have another sibling or two in my house, no! you wouldn't! I would swap with you any day, Zak.

Lee goes to get his sports bag, and his Mum is fussing around him, awww Mum, would you leave me alone, I'm only trying to brush your hair, she said, we're away now, wish us luck.

Good luck, boys! all the family are wishing the boys luck on their way out the door.

Lee closes the door behind him, thank god for that, thank god for what? Zak: asked? peace and quiet away from my family, they aren't that bad, surely? Zak replies! you're lucky, you're an only child, Zak, real lucky! I would love to have a Brother or Sister, even both.

It's a bit lonely on your own. I'll swap you any day Zak, any day of the week.

Lee and Zak continue down the road when a car pulls over beside them, do you want a lift, boys? the boys look up, and they see Ronan Powell with his head stuck out the back window, yeah, thanks Ronan.

It's getting a bit cold here now, said Zak. the boys jump in and a deep voice says hello, they both look, and it's Ronan's dad, a big burly man with loads of facial hair, hello sir, said Zak, call me fearghal, sir is very formal, just plain fearghal, the three boys in the back seat start talking, and Ronan tells the other 2 that his dad played in spain for athletic bilbao, years and years ago, he played in midfield, only played 12 times, as he got injured and had to retire.

He must have been good, Lee asks. he was, but he was only 22 Mum said he was struck down before he got going.  Does he give you any tips, Ronan? well, he is a bookmaker and that's his job. the boys start to laugh out loud, and Ronan's Dad asks them: what's so funny? nothing dad, I was just telling them what you do for a living, awww that's ok son, you have to make a living somehow.

What odds would you give your son, is Ronan going to score today? asks lee.

I would give you even money, he'll get 1 today, maybe 2. says Ronan's Dad, Ronan has a big silly smile on his face, when lee smirks and says, be hard to score from the bench, sir! the boys are killing themselves with laughter in the back seat.

Ronan's Dad speaks out and says, he'll get a run out today, fresh legs up front, you'll see lads, you'll see, the car pulls up outside the school, the boys jump out and thank Mr. Powell

For the lift, not a bother, boys, good luck today and give that rovers team a good thrashing today, Mr. Powell then drives off and repeats himself, give them a good trashing today, boys. the boys go in the main gate.

The away bus is already parked in the car park, Zak looks up, and the first player he sees, is the big number 5 from oakheart Rovers, donkey! Zak has history with this boy, he always seems to kick Zak and no one else, (Zak got a rough time at national school, the older boys always seemed to pick on him) he points at Zak and makes a gesture with his eyes, meaning I'll be watching you, Zak just smiles back and waves to him, (I'm getting tired of this, Zak mutters under his breath) donkey's face turns from smirking to annoyance, the match hasn't even started yet, but already, Zak and donkey have started to wind each other up, the boys go into the home changing rooms and Mr. Wright is standing by the door, he stops Zak on the way in and pulls him aside, I need to speak with you after the game.

Don't let me forget, can you make sure to remind me? thanks son, now go get changed, Zak said ok but found that conservation a bit strange, Mr. Wright starts his team talk as kick-off is approaching, I don't want you to think of this as a derby game,i want you to think of this as your opportunity.

It's your time to make it happen, today! you can create this opportunity, let's get out there and make it happen.

The team are roaring and are charged up for the derby game, they all leave the changing room and run out to the pitch.

The game is a close affair and nothing can separate this derby. 78 minutes on the clock, and both managers make a few changes, Ronan Powell, Stephen Kane and Paul Tierney all come on for Tyrone Reilly, David Ryan and Gary Rice.

Stephen Kane wins the ball and launches a long ball up the pitch, the voice comes again, get to the edge of the box, hold off the defender and turn right, then left.

Zak Brady has his back to the Rovers goal and his eyes are fixed on the ball that seems to be stuck in the sky for an age,  the ball comes down and Zak takes it on his chest, he is holding the big number 5 off, and as he turns into the box, Zak hears the voice again, hold him off, turn right, then turn left.

Zak turns to the right, the defender has his arms all over him, then Zak quickly turns left, and as he slips past the defender, he is too quick for him and the big number 5 that is nicknamed donkey, pulls Zak to the ground, and the referee blows the whistle and points to the spot, penalty! the Rovers' defenders crowd around the referee and in the melee, a red card is shown, number 5 from Oakheart Rovers is sent off, he was sent off for pushing the referee.

Zak Brady picks up the ball and walks towards the penalty spot, he stops, just before the penalty spot, and turns to the sub Ronan Powell, gives him the ball, make your Dad proud! Ronan Powell puts the ball on the spot.

The referee blows his whistle, Powell steps up and smashes the ball into the roof of the net, the keeper is standing on his line, he hasn't moved, the sheer power has beaten him all ends up.

Rovers restart the game, and paul tierney wins the ball back and passes to Noah, Noah beats 1 defender, then another, the voice comes again, get to the penalty spot, Zak runs into the box, and Noah whips in the cross, Zak meets it and powers his header towards goal, the keeper is beaten, the ball hits the post, and Ronan Powell is following up to get his second goal of the game, it's 2-0, Lee lifts Ronan up in the air, your Dad was spot on! Are you sure he's a bookmaker? I would say he's a psychic, imagine predicting you scoring two today, unbelievable! Rovers kick-off and the whistle goes, the game is over.

As the team celebrate, Zak looks over to the touchline and sees Jack and Sarah Jessica waving to him, he jogs over but he can't see anyone, he says to himself that was strange, all players are going to the changing rooms when mr wright pulls Zak to the side, great game Zak, I have some news for you, Sarah Jessica is awake, and she's asking for you. What? She's awake? I thought she was in a coma.

She's pulled through, and the surgeons think it's a miracle! Mr. Wright goes on to say, it seems she is now clear of cancer, she's sitting up, talking away and wants you to visit her. Zak is smiling from ear to ear, I'll just get changed and head over.

# CHAPTER 9
## *Time's up?*

Zak arrives at the hospital and runs up the three flights of stairs to room 217, he walks in, looks up and see's Sarah Jessica surrounded by her parents and friends. come in, Zak, ingrid says, Zak comes over closer and gives Sarah Jessica a big hug, they hug for an age, and both of them share happy tears.

Coach dempsey tells Sarah Jessica that they are going for a coffee and ask, does she want anything back? no thanks, Dad, I have some juice here, the Dempsey leave the room, Zak starts to ask Sarah Jessica some questions, what happened? I thought you were in a coma.

Are you all clear now? Will it come back? slow down, Zak! I'm going to be alright, I was in a coma, but I'm wide awake now!the cancer may come back, but I've been giving a clean bill of health for now. with a tear in his eyes, Zak holds Sarah Jessica's hand and says, I am so relieved that you are going to be alright.

I hate to imagine my life without you, when we scored the second goal today, I looked over and saw you standing beside Jack, Jack? Who is Jack? Sarah Jessica asks.

Oh, did I not tell you about Jack, no, you didn't, Sarah Jessica said, when i am on the pitch, I always hear the same voice, he tells me to go here, go there, I always end up at the right place and always seem to score.

Sarah Jessica asks, who is this boy? Have you told anyone else? people might think you are going mad.

Zak starts to laugh, I have told Lee and no one else. he thinks I'm going mad, do you think I'm mad? Sarah Jessica doesn't answer, Do you think I'm going mad? no, but it does sound very iffy, I mean, a boy who speaks to you from the sideline, is He a ghost? it is a bit stretched, Zak puts his hand on his heart, I'm telling you the truth, he starts to tell Sarah Jessica the whole story, from the start.

Sarah Jessica sits straight up on the bed and is showing real interest, she is staring at Zak with her big blue eyes, Zak keeps talking, and then Sarah Jessica says, I'm really glad that you are here with me today, you are the only person i want to talk to, Zak blushes and goes bright red, Sarah Jessica teases Zak, and they both laugh out loud, gazing into each other's eyes.

They continue to talk for hours until the matron comes in to tell everyone to go home, you can visit tomorrow, Sarah Jessica has to get her rest, you can say your goodbye but you must go now.

Zak holds Sarah Jessica's hand and tells her that he thought her time was up, and i'm so grateful that you are here and well. I can't wait to see you tomorrow, me too, says Sarah Jessica.

Zak kisses Sarah Jessica on the lips, Are we still on for the cinema?

We can share the popcorn! Sarah Jessica smiles and says you said the magic word.

Zak laughs, kisses Sarah Jessica again and says goodnight honey, see you tomorrow. I can't wait! replies Sarah Jessica.

Zak and the dempsey's leave the room, waving to Sarah Jessica as they go out the door. Justin Dempsey tells Zak that he is happy for him to see his Daughter anytime, Zak's face bursts into a big smile and says cool! they all leave together, and Zak gets a lift home with the Dempsey's. Zak has been busy visiting sarah jessica these past 2 Months, she will be finally allowed to go home tomorrow, Coach Dempsey asks Zak if he is ready to play today against Sliabh Rua, 100 percent coach, canny wait.

Oakheart Celtic are unbeaten in months and find themselves, 3 points clear, the match is delayed as there is a clash of kits.

Sliabh Rua has been kitted out in red and white stripes, with the home team wearing red and white hoops, Sliabh Rua doesn't have another kit to wear, so Oakheart changed into their second kit, yellow and navy hoops.

The game finally kicks off, and it's the home team that attack down the left, Celtic's Winger skips past a couple of defenders and sends in a first time cross, the forward flicks the ball on, and Noah is steaming in at the far post to cushion his header into the far corner of the net, oakheart go 1 up after a minute.

Finn makes it 2 nil after 7 minutes as he lobs the keeper, Finn scores again after 18 minutes, a one-two with Lee, bamboozles the Sliabh Rua number 2 it's 3-0. the home side have a corner and Zak hears Jack's voice, stand in front of the keeper, Zak moves into the box and Jack whispers again, stand in front of the keeper.

The corner is driven in hard from Finn, Zak gets their first, just ahead of the keeper, who was ready to catch the ball, Zak's glancing header - down beats everyone, and he makes it 4-0 just before the break.

The whistle blows, and as both teams head in for a 15-minute break, Zak hears the voice again, he immediately glances over at the touchline but doesn't see anyone. he hears Jack's voice again, and looks all around, he spots Jack O'Leary sitting beside the nets, Zak jog's over,

Zak: what do you think of the game? Jack: very good.

Zak: Can you explain why you're talking to me today?

Jack: my time here is nearly up!

Zak: what do you mean, time's nearly up? Jack: you'll see,

Zak: I don't know what you mean.

Why did you appear to me?

Why can't you stay?

Jack: I'm just here to help you. Zak is left puzzled, Jack gets up and starts to walk away,

Zak: Where are you going? and are you coming back?

Jack: I will, we'll talk again.

Jack disappears in an instant. Zak puts his hands on his hips, shakes his head and walks off towards the changing rooms. The second half gets underway and Oakheart continue where they left off, Finn makes it 5-0, he bags himself a hat-trick.

Noah scores the 6th, Lee heads in his first and Oakheart's 7th, the match finishes with another header from Lee, 8-0. it's the biggest win of the campaign, Mr. Wright praises the boys, saying that's the best 90 minutes of football I've seen since I came to the school. he went on to say that Justin, (Coach Dempsey) would be back for the last 6 games. There were a few groans and sigh but the majority were happy.

Zak and Lee were walking home, Zak: I spoke to Jack today at half time, Lee: Where?

Zak: beside the goals.

Lee: What did he say?

Zak: that he wouldn't be around much longer,

Lee: Where is he going?

Zak: Don't know?

Lee: you do sound a little bit crazy, Zak.

Zak: I don't care, I don't care how it sounds, Zak is getting very irritated with Lee.

Lee: I kinda half believe you, but I would need some proof, can I meet Jack and chat with him too? Zak: sure! but you can't tell anyone about this! Lee: deadly, I won't tell a soul.

# CHAPTER 10
## *Answers*

1. Oakheart Celtic 60
2. Mountmear 57
3. Scarton 54
4. Oakheart Rovers 53
5. Dun Mount 50

With only 3 games to go, the School's League was coming to an exciting end, four teams were battling it out, and with all 4 playing each other this weekend, no one could predict this year's winner. The leaders were away to Mountmear, Coach Dempsey was giving his final instructions, the team left the changing rooms and entered the pitch, Zak was looking all around this compact Stadium, the fans seem to be so close to the touchline, It was a very intimidating atmosphere and not many teams left here with 3 points.

In fact, only 2 teams won here in the last 20 years, dun mount and Oakheart Rovers. Mountmear kicked off and attacked down Celtic's right, the cross comes in, and the number 8 gets a head to the ball and it flashes off the bar.

Early warning for Oakheart, the game ebbs and flows, and the green and white stripes come down the right-hand side again, the left-back is getting a torrid time in the first 30 minutes, the winger is getting so much joy and sends in another cross, again, the number 8 gets a header towards the goal but Kennedy is in goal catches this one.

Coach Dempsey is shouting instructions to his winger, to get back and help out his defender, half time comes and the teams go in 0-0, Justin Dempsey makes a change and tweaks a few things in defence.

Ronan Powell comes on for Tyrone Reilly, and it's Powell who gets the first chance of the second half he shoots from 30 yards, and the big Mountmear keeper touches the ball round the post.

Zak hears the voice, go to the edge of the box, edge of the box, the ball is whipped into the back post, Mountmear clear their lines, the voice again says, go to the edge of the box, the ball comes to Zak, who meets it on the half volley and rifles it into the bottom corner, the visitor's lead against the run of play, Zak spots Jack O'Leary on the touchline and gives him a nod, Jack smiles and waves back. Mountmear attack for the last 30 minutes and are repaid for their efforts as the number 11 gets past celtic's left back again and shoots first time past Oakheart's keeper, the ball goes in off the post, and the keeper is beaten at his near side, Coach Dempsey has his hands on top of his head, he can't believe it. Mountmear keep attacking, and the Oakheart fans are calling for the whistle to end this game. Mountmear shoots from the edge of the box but it sails over the bar.

The ref blows his whistle, the match finished 1-1. this result keeps Celtic ahead by 3 points, with two games left and their rivals, Oakheart Rovers playing mountmear in their final game, could they do them a favour? the weeks are flying in, and it's nearly the end of term, Zak spends most of his time at school, talking and hanging out with Sarah Jessica, Zak? yes, Sarah Jessica? I know who your ghost is! Who? Who is he? How do you know him? he's an uncle of my dad's, the look on Zak's face is a mixture of bemusement and shock. but I asked the coach Months ago!

Zak said, he didn't realise himself but he was looking through some old photos, when he came across this photo.

Sarah Jessica shows Zak an old photo of a boy with a football, my granny had these stored away in her attic. He looks identical to the boy on the touchline, Zak said. Granny told dad that the boy was his uncle, oh my god! Sarah Jessica you're related to the ghost? yeah, I kinda am, I wonder? Why is he appearing now and to you, Zak? Has anyone else seen him? I haven't seen him and I'm supposed to be related to him! well, when I see him next, I'm going to ask him a few questions.

I still don't understand why he's helping me. Why not help Lee, Finn or Noah? you must need the help more, Laughed Sarah Jessica, ha ha, very funny, funny and beautiful so you are, I'm the luckiest boy in the whole world, oh, yes you are, Zak Brady! you are one lucky boy, the bell rings, and it's double maths next for Zak.

Zak and sarah jessica continue talking, when Ms. Stapleton walks by, come along you two, plenty of time for chit chat later, it's maths time, time to get your brain working, Zak lets out a loud sigh! I know it's your favourite subject, Zak.

Ms .Stapleton smiles as she walks into the classroom.

I'll see you later Zak, Sarah Jessica kisses him on the cheek and goes to her class.

Zak slowly walks to his seat, Zak! Ms. Stapleton shouts! I know you dislike maths, maybe as much as I dislike Football, but It's time for you to get the head down as the exams start in 2 weeks.

Ok miss, Zak replied all he could think about, was how jack was related to Sarah Jessica? He was looking forward to the next match, which was in a few days, so, he could ask Jack all these questions that were going around in his head.

The bell sounds for the end of the school day, Zak meets up with Lee to tell him all about what he discovered about Jack, Lee doesn't really believe it, but Zak is adamant.

I'm going to ask him at the game against the Blackhawks, you can come too. Excellent, replied Lee. look forward to meeting your ghost, woooooooooo! Lee starts laughing, maybe I'll change my mind, Zak says.

I'm only messing mate, not funny, Lee, not funny at all. They walk out the school gate and board their bus, Sarah Jessica waves at Zak through the window, see you tomorrow! Zak gets closer to the window and waves back at Sarah Jessica, he is besotted with her and his heart jumps every time he sees her.

Sit down, you big drip! you're just jealous, Lee, no girl would look at you! the boys tease each other the whole way home, they both get off at their houses, they say their goodbyes and go home. saturday comes and Zak Isn't feeling so good, he travels to the school but tells Coach Dempsey that he has very little energy, that's no problem Zak.

I'll get Ronan to take your place, the match is well into the second half, where Oakheart Celtic are well on top, when a long ball goes over the defence, the number 9 for Blackhawks is on it in a flash, he drives forward into the box and is one-on-one with the Oakheart Celtic keeper.

He goes past him with ease but in a desperate attempt to get the ball, Oakheart's keeper pulls the Blackhawks number 9, to the ground, he still has part of his shirt in his hands,.

The referee points to the spot and blows his whistle, penalty! out of nothing.

The away side have a great chance here, Blackhawks number 9 gets up, grabs the ball and places it on the spot. he waits for the whistle and takes 3 steps back. the ref blows his whistle and the number 9 side foots the ball into the middle of the net, the team leading the league are behind. Things go from bad to worse as Celtic's number four is sent off for an off-the-ball incident.

Ronan Powell limps off in the last minute to add more misery for Oakheart.

It's full time. Blackhawks have won 1-0. News quickly filters in that the second-place team Mountmear have won 4-1 at home to cadden city. The league table is as close as it has ever been with only 1 game remaining.

1. Oakheart Celtic 61 37
2. Mountmear 61 36
3. Oakheart Rovers 59 30
4. Scarton 57 24
5. Blackhawks 56 19

The last fixtures see second playing third, Oakheart Rovers are at home to Mountmear, where Oakheart Celtic will go to forest Celtic, Oakheart Celtic are level with Mountmear but have a goal difference of plus 1 better than their rivals Mountmear.

Zak looks around the pitch after the game for any sight of Jack, but there's no one left on the field, everyone is long gone, and Zak is a little disappointed not to have seen Jack, he has a few questions for him.

Zak! Zak! Zak looks around and can see his Dad, Roy, waving to him.

Yes Dad, I'm here to pick you up, your mum said you weren't feeling well, thanks Dad, I'll just grab my coat from the changing room.

Zak walks in, and the team is totally silent, Zak looks around and can see the coach just staring at the team, he has a look in his eyes that every player knows, not to say a word, just stay silent, don't speak or move. Zak grabs his coat and waves to the other boys, he jumps into the car, and his dad asks, what was the score? we got beat, 1-0, Dad.ah well, son, you can't win them all.

Roy turns on the radio and starts to sing. they drive for home as the evening comes to a close. a few days pass, and Zak bumps into Sarah Jessica in the school corridor, she was crying. What's the matter? Zak asked, It's nothing Zak, I'll be ok.

Just tell me what's making you feel like this, it's my mum and dad, What's wrong with them? they are breaking up! they are getting a divorce! I am so sorry, Sarah Jessica! Is there anything I can do? no, you can't, but you can call over later and watch a film with me, I will, I'll bring the popcorn, they embrace in the corridor and walk to their next class.

The weekend rolls around again quickly and it's the final match of Celtic's league campaign. the boys board the bus and get ready for the 10-mile trip to forest Celtic.

They arrive at the ground, and it is surrounded by woodland. The boys can't get over how green everything is and they start to count the many trees lining the road. As they start to leave the bus and enter the ground, some of the boys are excited and some are nervous, Stephen Kane is making his first start today and is as green as the trees, he doesn't feel well and rushes to the bathroom.

Coach Dempsey lets out a hearty laugh and jokes, does anyone else want to join young Kane? alright lads, listen up! this is the last game, and you have been excellent all year, success is no accident, today i want you to go out and enjoy yourselves, play with smiles on your faces and get the 3 points.

Finally, "nothing is impossible" the game is only 12 minutes in when Noah hits an unstoppable shot from 22 yards into the far corner of the net.

The keeper never saw it coming. the home side are under the cosh in the first half, their keeper is making save after save. how this game is only 1-0,god only knows.

The whistle blows for half-time, and forest Celtic go in at halftime 1 nil down. all the boys are asking the score of the Mountmear game, Coach Dempsey checks his phone and says,1 nil to Mountmear, if things stay the same, then Oakheart Celtic will be champions.

The second half is well underway, and there is talk in the crowd saying a goal in the Mountmear game. word comes through that Mountmear have, indeed scored their second. If things stay the same, both teams will finish level on points and goals difference, that means as things stands, there will be a playoff for the league.

There are 2 minutes left on the clock, and the ball it is pinballing around the midfield. A wispy voice reaches Zak, stay on the halfway line, stay on the halfway line, the ball is booted high into the Oakheart Celtic half, all the forest Celtic team go in search of the equaliser, finn plays a one-two with lee and hits a 35-yard pass to Zak, who is standing all alone on the halfway line? the wispy voice calls again, go directly at the goals. directly at the goals.

Zak collects the ball and runs as fast as he can with the ball. He gets to the edge of the box when he sees the big keeper racing out of his nets. Zak sidesteps him and drags the ball to his left foot, the keeper slides past, and Zak has an empty goal, he runs on some more, then he passes the ball to his left hand side, Stephen Kane making his first start, has the easiest task of tapping the ball into the empty net, he runs away with his shirt over his head, Lee congratulates Zak, that was very unselfish of you, first start, first goal, we'll never hear the end of it now, he'll be hard to listen to, on the bus back.

That should be game over. minutes later, the referee blows for full-time. mountmear have won 2-0 too, but Oakheart have a better goal difference by 1 goal, and that's enough to make them champions. the team drop to their knees in pure euphoria, there are tears of joy and happiness, they did it.

They won the league, they are the champions, the team start heading for the changing rooms and as Zak walks off the pitch, he spots Jack in the corner of his eye, Zak jogs over to him, and he starts to ask the questions that have been running through his mind these past few months.

Why do you keep appearing to me?

Why are you helping me?

What happened to you?

Am I going mad?

You're not going mad! I had cancer, got it aged 11 and I died aged 15, I'm helping you because I heard your prayer, What? asked Zak. you prayed a long time ago, to be a good footballer in school and you wanted to win a trophy.

I would like to think that i have helped you. I'm really happy that you and sj are friends. My journey is over and I have to go back, I enjoyed my time here watching you develop.

Wait! Where are you going?

I've just met you! my time is up, Zak! my work is done! take care of yourself!

We might meet again. (Jack waves and walks away) wait Jack! I have more questions. Jack turns around, listen Zak! when i died, i went somewhere, I don't really know where, but I remember seeing you and sj, me and Sarah Jessica? Zak asks.

Yes, I saw you both, I also saw you lifting a big shiny cup in a Football Stadium, I also saw SJ on a hospital bed, but I also saw you together at the cinema, I have seen other things but I can't disclose anymore, What? will Sarah Jessica be ok? yes, Zak, she will be fine.

Take care of each other, I will see you again. Jack winks at zak and leaves the pitch again, wait Jack! just a few more questions! a misty fog descends all over the pitch, Zak is frantically looking around for Jack and when the fog lifts, Jack just disappears into thin air, gone in a flash. (Sarah Jessica runs up to Zak) congratulations, babe, well done today.

How are we going to celebrate tonight?

Hi honey, We can do anything you want, you just missed Jack, Jack? your ghost? asked Sarah Jessica, yeah, my ghost, Jack O'Leary. (Zak and Sarah Jessica  walk around the pitch holding hands, they talk, kiss and laugh for ages) (Zak looks all around him, looks up to the sky and says) I really hope to see you again, thanks, Jack.

# The End

# The Ghost of Zak Brady

## Ciaran McLaughlin

My name is Ciaran McLaughlin. I was born in Buncrana, Co. Donegal, Ireland. I have been employed in a kitchen manufacturing factory for the past 20 years. I am 52 years old. I have been married to Majella for the last 24 years. I have 4 children, 3 boys and I girl. I really enjoy writing and have written some unpublished short stories in different genres. I love reading, walking, jogging and listening to music. I love sports, football, and golf (I am a member of Buncrana Golf Club, handicap of 8). I am also a member of Greasepaint Productions. ( Drama, singing and theatre group ) I am currently in the process of writing my second book (untitled).

9 781964 331072